To Sheila Barry, with gratitude for a decade of
life-changing conversations. JABL

To my parents, who still hang my drawings on
their wall. NN

Text copyright © 2017 by JonArno Lawson
Illustrations copyright © 2017 by Natalie Nelson
Published in Canada and the USA in 2017 by Groundwood Books

All rights reserved. No part of this publication may be reproduced, stored
in a retrieval system or transmitted, in any form or by any means, without
the prior written consent of the publisher or a license from The Canadian
Copyright Licensing Agency (Access Copyright). For an Access Copyright
license, visit www.accesscopyright.ca or call toll free to 1-800-893-5777.

Groundwood Books / House of Anansi Press
groundwoodbooks.com

We acknowledge for their financial support of our publishing program
the Canada Council for the Arts, the Ontario Arts Council and the
Government of Canada

Library and Archives Canada Cataloguing in Publication
Lawson, JonArno, author
Uncle Holland / JonArno Lawson ; illustrated by Natalie Nelson.
Issued in print and electronic formats.
ISBN 978-1-55498-929-4 (hardback). — ISBN 978-1-55498-930-0 (pdf)
I. Nelson, Natalie, illustrator II. Title.
PS8573.A93U63 2017   jC813'.54   C2016-904120-4
C2016-904121-2

The artwork in this book was rendered
in digital collage, incorporating found
photography and ink drawings.
Design by Michael Solomon
Printed and bound in Malaysia

Canada Council
for the Arts

Conseil des Arts
du Canada

ONTARIO ARTS COUNCIL
CONSEIL DES ARTS DE L'ONTARIO

an Ontario government agency
un organisme du gouvernement de l'Ontario

With the participation of the Government of Canada
Avec la participation du gouvernement du Canada | Canadä

UNCLE HOLLAND

JonArno Lawson

illustrated by
NATALIE NELSON

GROUNDWOOD BOOKS
HOUSE OF ANANSI PRESS
TORONTO   BERKELEY

Palmer and Ella had three sons — Holland, Jimmy and Ivan. Jimmy and Ivan were good boys, but Holland, who was the eldest, was always getting into trouble.

PALMER ELLA

HOLLAND

JIMMY

IVAN

Holland sometimes stole things. He liked stuff that was pretty, and sometimes he couldn't help stuffing that pretty stuff into his pockets.

One day, when the police had caught Holland for the thirty-seventh time, they said, "Holland Lawson, either you go to jail or you join the army. It's up to you."

HOLLAND LAWSON,
EITHER YOU GO TO
JAIL OR YOU JOIN
THE ARMY.

IT'S UP TO YOU.

Holland's parents were heartbroken. His little brothers, Jimmy and Ivan, cried and cried. They would miss their big brother even though he stole their candy and their dimes.

Holland's father decided to spend the rest of his life watching his fish swim around in his fish tank.

"Fish can't disappoint me," he said.

But Holland's mother said, "Palmer, we have to be grateful. Holland may be a thief, but he's never been a liar."

Holland felt horrible. How could he ever make it up to his family?

Now what would you do if you were Holland? Would you go to jail, or join the army?

CHECK ONE.
☐ JAIL
☐ ARMY

Holland decided to join the army, and they sent him to a very pretty place far away to the south.

Now this place was full of all sorts of extraordinary things — but not the kinds of things you can put in your pockets. It had palm trees, parrots, flowers and big blue waves.

And what do you think lived in those big blue waves?

That's right —

FISH!

Holland had never seen such beautiful fish before. He wished so much that he could put them in his pockets — his father would love them.

Suddenly,
he had an idea. He
would go to the market and
buy — but definitely not steal — a little
paint palette and a block of paper.
Then, with everything set the way he
liked it, he would paint the fish.

On weekends, when Holland had leave, he would go to the market and sell his pictures.

In a short while he was able to send his parents
a big wad of cash, along with a beautiful picture of
the extraordinary fish, which his father hung up
behind his fish tank.

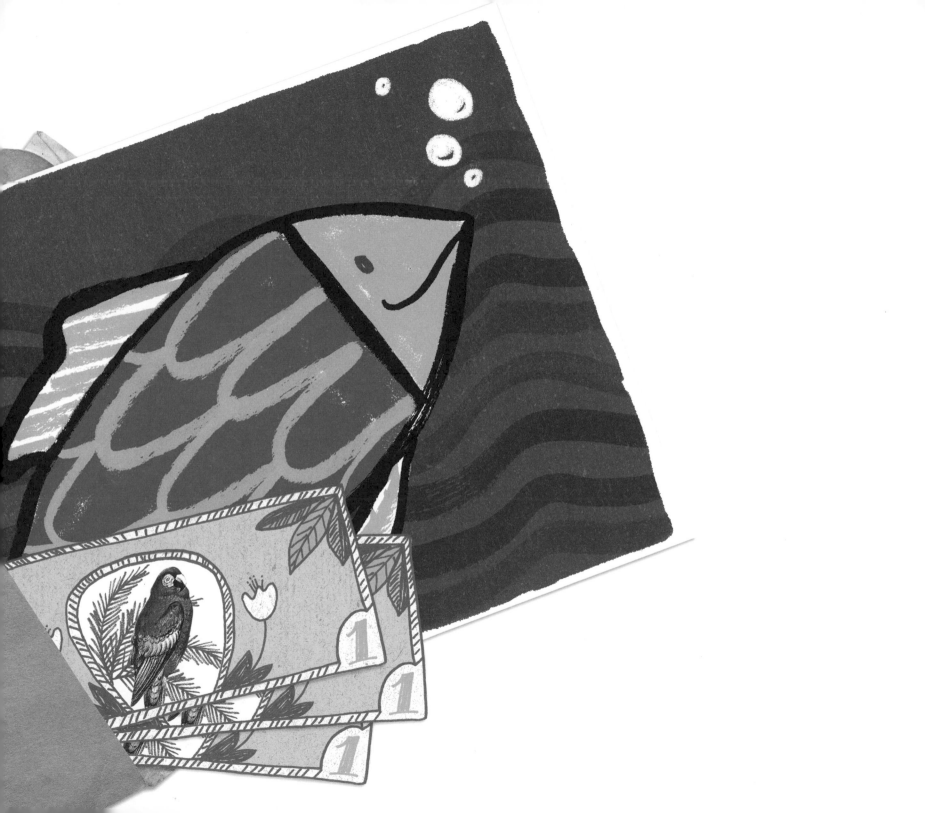

His parents, though, were worried about the money. Was Holland stealing again?

His father wrote him a letter:

Holland,
dear son, you're
sometimes a thief,
but you've never
been a liar.
Tell me now —
did you earn the
money honestly?

And Holland, who knew they would
be worried, wrote back:

DEAR MAMA AND PAPA,

NOT EVERYTHING THAT'S
PRETTY CAN BE STUFFED IN
YOUR POCKETS!

DON'T FRET — I'VE LEARNED
HOW TO PUT PRETTY THINGS
INTO PICTURES AND SELL
THEM INSTEAD!

YOUR SON IN THE SUNSHINE,
HOLLAND

And so Palmer and Ella knew they didn't have to worry anymore about Holland. And even Jimmy and Ivan stopped crying.

AUTHOR'S NOTE

AShley 2-8641

Holland B. Lawson
Manufacturing Jeweler and Engraver
HAND ENGRAVING · DESIGNING
EXPERT DIAMOND SETTING · REMOUNTING
JEWELRY REPAIR · SPECIAL ORDER WORK

5 Broadway   (Room 514)   Troy, New York

At all family occasions, stories were told about my uncle Holland, who got into (and out of) a lot of trouble during his short life. He really did start out as a soldier, but ended up as a jeweler. My extended family — the Livingston Avenue Lawsons of Albany, New York — were more numerous than they appear to be in this story. In real life they were Palmer, Ella, Birdsall, Townsend, Adrian, Langdon, Holland, Jean, Cornie, Jimmy and Ivan — and all of them were artists.

Special thanks to Simone Bender for providing the forum that made this story possible.